The Mystery
of the
Missing
Finger

Written by Josh Lacey
Illustrated by Jim Field

Published by Pearson Education Limited, Edinburgh Gate, Harlow, Essex, CM20 2JE
Registered company number: 872828

www.pearsonschools.co.uk

Text © Josh Lacey 2011

Designed by Bigtop
Original illustrations © Pearson Education 2011
Illustrated by Jim Field

The right of Josh Lacey to be identified as author of this work has been asserted
by him in accordance with the Copyright, Designs and Patents Act 1988.

First published 2011

15
10 9 8 7

British Library Cataloguing in Publication Data

A catalogue record for this book is available from the British Library

ISBN 978 0 435 91520 9

Printed and bound in China by CTPS

Acknowledgements
We would like to thank the children and teachers of Bangor Central Integrated
Primary School, NI; Bishop Henderson C of E Primary School, Somerset;
Brookside Community Primary School, Somerset; Cheddington Combined School,
Buckinghamshire; Cofton Primary School, Birmingham; Dair House Independent
School, Buckinghamshire; Deal Parochial School, Kent; Newbold Riverside Primary
School, Rugby and Windmill Primary School, Oxford for their invaluable help in
the development and trialling of the Bug Club resources.

Every effort has been made to contact copyright holders of material reproduced
in this book. Any omissions will be rectified in subsequent printings if notice is
given to the publishers.

Contents

Chapter 1   5

Chapter 2   11

Chapter 3   20

Chapter 4   27

Chapter 5   31

Chapter 6   36

Chapter 7   44

This is the story of a priceless painting and a stately home and a thief with a missing finger, but all those things come later. Before anything else, it's the story of a boy named Matt Clarke who couldn't speak French.

He didn't even want to speak French. Given the choice, he would just have spoken English. But he wasn't given the choice. He was only eleven years old and his parents made those kinds of decisions for him.

This is what they decided. That summer holiday, Matt would spend two weeks with a girl named Véronique.

Véronique was French, you see, and her parents wanted her to improve her English. She would come to England for a week and stay with the Clarkes, then Matt would stay with Véronique's family in France and speak nothing but French. After a fortnight, they would each be fluent in the other's language.

That was the idea, anyway.

Now it was the second Saturday in August and Matt was at the airport with his mum and dad, waiting for Véronique. He stared at the faces of arriving travellers, wondering which one was her.

That
tall
girl
with
her hair
in bunches?

That tubby girl
with tattoos?

That small girl
with the round face
and round glasses
and a very
determined
expression?

Yes – that was her. The small girl marched straight up to Mrs Clarke, who was holding a piece of cardboard with big black letters reading VERONIQUE PETIT.

"Good afternoon," said the small girl in a strong French accent. "You are Mr and Mrs Clarke? And Mathieu? I am here for staying with you, yes?"

"Are you Véronique?" asked Mrs Clarke.

"Of course," said the small girl as if she had never heard such a silly question.

"It's very nice to meet you," said Mrs Clarke. "I'm Camilla and this is Colin. And here's Matthew."

"*Enchanté!*" said Véronique, darting forwards and giving Matt a kiss on each cheek. He tried to dodge out of the way, but she was too quick for him.

In the car on the way home, Véronique talked incessantly. She discussed her flight and her suitcase and the other travellers and the differences between England and France. "My father, he say to me, the food in your country is very bad. This is true?"

"I don't really know," said Mrs Clarke, who was already beginning to wonder if this whole thing had been a terrible mistake. "What do you think, Colin?"

"I like English food," said Mr Clarke. "But, then, I am English."

"I will cook for you," said Véronique. "Then you will see what is good food. I will cook cassoulet, perhaps. You like cassoulet?"

Mr and Mrs Clarke confessed that they had never tasted cassoulet. Véronique was shocked. Her mind was made up. Before the end of the week, she would make it for them.

Matt wondered what cassoulet might be, but he didn't ask. He knew it would only make him look stupid.

On Sunday morning, Mr and Mrs Clarke asked Véronique how she would like to spend her first full day in England.

Véronique replied immediately, "I wish to see a house."

"We're in a house already," said Matt.

"A real English house," explained Véronique.

"This *is* a real English house."

"A house like in the films, you know? A real English country house."

"You mean a stately home!" said Mr Clarke. "Well, that shouldn't be a problem. We could go to Marchmont Hall."

Matt groaned. He hated traipsing around boring old stately homes. "I'll stay here," he said, but he knew his parents wouldn't let him.

When they arrived at Marchmont Hall, Mr Clarke bought tickets for everyone. Then he led them through a tall stone gateway and up the gravel path to the house.

A large wooden notice was fixed to the wall beside the entrance. Véronique read it slowly to herself.

WELCOME TO MARCHMONT HALL

Marchmont Hall is one of the finest stately homes in the British Isles. The original house was built in 1532 by Tobias Sprockett, the first Duke of Marchmont, and the family have lived here ever since.

The Duke and Duchess hope that you enjoy your visit and ask you to remember that this is a private house. Please do not touch the paintings or sit on the chairs.

Marchmont Hall is open to the public on the second Sunday of every month.

There are guided tours every hour from 11.00am – 6.00pm.

Cream teas are served in the pantry 3.00pm – 5.00pm.

Véronique turned to Matt. "You must tell me, Mathieu, what is *cream teas*?"

"It's scones and jam and cream," said Matt. "And tea, if you like it, which I don't."

"This is typical of the English cuisine?"

"I suppose so."

"Then I must take it."

Véronique was determined to sample some real English cooking.

Inside the house, an elderly lady with grey hair and a blue woolly cardigan was perched on a wooden chair. "Good morning," she said. "Could I see your tickets, please? Thank you, dear. That's perfect. The tour starts through that door on your left."

When the Clarkes and Véronique trooped through the door on the left, they discovered that a small group had already assembled. There were two American tourists with cameras hanging round their necks, a Dutch couple in matching yellow raincoats and a large bearded Australian wearing baggy shorts and flipflops.

After several "good mornings" and a single "g'day", everyone settled down to wait for the guide.

A moment later, an energetic old lady appeared in the doorway. "Hello, you must be my eleven o'clock," she said in a cheery voice. "Will you follow me, please?"

The guide knew a thousand facts about Marchmont Hall and she shared them with anyone within earshot.

"Now we come to my favourite part of the Hall," her voice boomed out. "I always feel that walking past these beautiful paintings is like walking through history."

Along the wall, there was a row of huge paintings in ornate gold frames, one of each of the nineteen dukes. The first duke

was a plump chap with a bright red face. A sword was strapped to his side and his right hand rested on a small statue of a deer standing on its hind legs. In many ways, the nineteenth duke resembled his ancestors – he had the same chubby cheeks and the same red nose – but, in the painting, he was wearing a dark suit, a white shirt and a neat blue tie.

From the gallery, the guide led them through the bedrooms, down the little staircase at the back of the house and into the kitchen. One wall was taken up by an enormous oven, big enough to roast a pig's head or half a sheep, and huge silver saucepans were stacked on the shelves.

"It is like the restaurant of my father," said Véronique. "But his restaurant, it is more clean."

They walked through the interlocking rooms of the ground floor and came to the drawing-room with its huge fireplace and long white sofas. Paintings hung on the walls and shelves held ancient leather-bound books.

"This is the last room on the tour," said the guide, "and, in many ways, the most fascinating. Hidden within these walls there is a secret panel concealing a priest hole. Does anyone know what a priest hole is?"

A couple of people nodded and raised their hands, but not Matt. He wasn't interested in priest holes; he was just relieved to hear that the tour was almost over. He looked for the exit, waiting for the moment when he could escape.

That was when he saw the thief.

3

Matt didn't know immediately that he was looking at a thief. He just knew he was looking at a man in a black mask. But why would anyone cover his face with a black mask unless he was a thief?

Matt wondered whether he should shout out a warning to all the others, who were busy looking at the priest hole.

But what if the man in the mask wasn't a thief at all? What if he had an illness which meant he had to wear a mask over his face at all times? How horrible – wherever he went, people would shout "Thief!" when in fact he was just an ordinary man with, for instance, an allergy to sunlight.

That was when Matt noticed the man's missing finger.

He was wearing black gloves. On his right hand, he had a thumb and four fingers. But on his left hand, the little finger of his glove was hanging loose.

Just as Matt was wondering how you might lose your little finger, the man in the mask darted across the room to a painting of a man and a horse. He reached up, grabbed the picture with both hands and lifted it from the wall. Immediately, an alarm went off, filling the air with a high-pitched screech.

The man in the mask turned around
slowly and faced the room as if he were
waiting for everyone to look at him.
Which was exactly what they did.

Apart from the man in the mask, there were ten people in the room: Matt, Véronique, Mr Clarke, Mrs Clarke, the Dutch couple, the Americans, the Australian and the guide. If they had acted together and moved fast, they could have grabbed the thief and wrestled him to the ground.

But no one moved.

The thief didn't move either. He just turned from side to side, looking at everyone in the room as if he wanted to memorise their faces.

The guide suddenly remembered her duties. At the top of her voice, she screamed: "You are not allowed to touch the pictures! Put that back right now!"

It was as if a spell had been broken. Without even thinking, Matt darted forwards, followed swiftly by Véronique and the bearded Australian. But the man in the mask was too fast for them. He sprinted across the room and, not hesitating for a moment, swung himself out of a window.

By the time Matt, Véronique and the Australian reached the window, the thief was disappearing down the drive with the painting under his arm.

"I don't believe it," cried the guide. "He's taken The Blind Horseman!"

"What's The Blind Horseman?" asked Matt.

"The Blind Horseman is the most valuable painting in Marchmont Hall. It was valued last year at nine million pounds. And now it's been stolen!"

The alarm was connected directly to the local police station. Within minutes, five police cars swept up the gravel drive, their sirens wailing, and uniformed officers swarmed into the house. They cordoned off Marchmont Hall, preventing anyone from entering or leaving, but they could find no sign of the thief or The Blind Horseman.

Detective Inspector Alan Stamp took charge of the investigation. He ordered his officers to round up everyone in the house.

The visitors, the owners, the staff – he wanted to talk to all of them.

First, Inspector Stamp interviewed the ten people who had been in the drawing-room when the thief struck. One after another, everyone told him the same curious detail: the thief was missing the little finger on his left hand.

Next, Inspector Stamp summoned the butler, the cook, the housemaids, the gardeners, the tour guides and the ticket collectors. He asked the Duke and Duchess to join them, too.

Once they were all gathered in the drawing room, the inspector noticed something very interesting: the butler was missing the little finger on his left hand.

The Clarkes walked back to their car.

Matt was walking a few paces behind the others, lost in thought. He should have been delighted to be leaving Marchmont Hall, but he couldn't stop thinking about the robbery.

Under questioning, the butler had explained that, three years ago, while he was sharpening a carving knife, he had chopped off his own little finger. This was enough to convince Inspector Stamp that he had found the thief. He dismissed the other witnesses, simply asking them to leave their names and addresses so the police could get in touch if they had any further questions.

Matt thought about the black mask and the gloves and The Blind Horseman and the thief's missing finger. Then he muttered, "It doesn't make sense."

He had really been talking to himself, but Véronique heard him. "What do you mean, Mathieu?"

"Oh, nothing," said Matt.

"If it is nothing, you do not say it. Tell me, what do you mean, *it doesn't make sense*?"

Matt didn't want to explain, but he knew Véronique wouldn't leave him alone till he told her everything. "If you were the butler, would you really steal that picture in front of so many people? Wouldn't you know you were going to get caught?"

"Perhaps he is stupid."

"No one's that stupid. And there's another thing. After he grabbed the painting from the wall, he didn't run for the exit. No, he stood there for a moment, turning very slowly from side to side. At the time, I thought he was looking at everyone in the room, memorising their faces. But I think he was actually giving *us* a chance to look at *him*."

"But why?"

"So we would notice his missing finger."

"Ah!" Véronique smiled. "The butler, he has been ... how do you say?"

"Framed!"

"Yes, the poor man, he has been framed. What can we do to help him?"

Matt noticed that Véronique said 'we' rather than 'you', but he didn't question it. He just shrugged his shoulders. "We can't do anything."

"Why not?"

"The police are here," said Matt. "They'll find the real thief."

"They think they have the thief already. They look no more. It is for us, Mathieu. We must find the real thief."

"How can we do that?"

"It is simple," said Véronique. "We must follow the clues."

"Which clues?"

"If there is a thief, there must be clues."

"What about them?" whispered Matt, gesturing at his parents.

Véronique didn't answer. She just winked.

A moment later, Matt and Véronique turned around together and ran back to Marchmont Hall.

6

Matt and Véronique crouched behind a police car, staring at a half-open window.

That was the window that the thief had climbed out of. Several police were milling around under the window, searching for clues or fingerprints.

"Let's go this way," whispered Matt, pointing towards the trees.

"Why this way?" asked Véronique.

"Because that's where the thief went."

They darted away from the car and

hurried across the lawn, following the trail taken by the thief. Soon they reached the curve in the drive. From here, the thief could have gone in three different directions: up to the road, across the fields or into the stables.

"Someone wait for him here in a car, no?" said Véronique.

"I don't know," said Matt. He looked around. Something didn't feel right. Then he realised what it was. If you were a thief, you couldn't bring a car here. You would be stopped at the gates and told to park in the car park like everyone else. Unless the thief didn't have a car at all. Perhaps he had a bicycle. Or a horse. Or ... Ah! What if he didn't go anywhere? What if he stayed right here?

"Where do you go?" asked Véronique.

"Just having a look," said Matt, heading into the stables.

Once inside, his eyes took a moment to adjust to the gloom. Then he saw that he was standing in a narrow block with a row of stalls down one side. There weren't any horses, but the cobblestones were damp and the air smelled of hay.

Matt tried to imagine that he was a thief, running in here, carrying a valuable painting. What would he do? Where would he go?

First, you'd stop yourself looking like a thief.

You'd take off your mask. And your gloves.

Maybe they were still here.

Matt started searching the stalls and the floor and the bales of hay.

"What do you do?" asked Véronique.

Matt explained what he was looking for.

"I will help you," said Véronique. "I go this way?"

"Sure."

They walked in different directions. Suddenly Véronique said, "Oh! What is this?"

"What's what?" asked Matt.

"On my shoe. Something is stuck." She plucked a piece of tape from the bottom of her shoe.

"It looks like sticky tape," said Matt.

"Ah, yes, it is the tape."

She was about to throw it away when Matt said, "Let me see that."

"Why?" asked Véronique.

"Just let me see it."

Holding the tape by its corner, she handed it to him.

Matt stepped out of the stables and held the tape up to the light. He squinted. There seemed to be something printed on the tape. What was it? A small round symbol of some sort. Was it an animal? A deer? For some reason, it looked oddly familiar.

"What do you find?" asked Véronique.

He showed it to her. "I'm sure I've seen it before, but I can't remember where."

"I will tell you," said Véronique. "It is the Coat of Arms of the Duke of Marchmont."

"How do you know?"

"You are not listening to the guide?"

"No."

"Ah, but you must. She had much information. She tell us about the Coat of Arms. It is the deer, standing up, like this, on his back legs. You see it in the house, no?"

Matt nodded and smiled. Once again, he had to admit that Véronique was right.

Throughout Marchmont Hall – carved into the wooden bannister, added to the paintings – there were pictures of a deer standing on its hind legs. And he'd seen it somewhere else too. But where? And then he remembered.

"We've got to stop him," he said.

"Stop who?" asked Véronique.

Matt didn't answer. He was already running back down the drive to Marchmont Hall.

Véronique raced after him.

In the magnificent drawing-room of
Marchmont Hall, Inspector Stamp was
quizzing Herbert Maples. The Duke was
watching. A few police-officers were
kneeling on the floor, searching for clues.
Others were photographing the window
and the empty space on the wall where The
Blind Horseman had been hanging.

The inspector said, "If you don't tell us
where you've stashed the painting, we'll
have to continue these questions at the

station – and I'm sure you don't want to do that."

"It is a matter of complete indifference to me," said the butler, "since I cannot possibly tell you anything which might help your investigation."

"Very well." The inspector nodded to one of his men. "Take him to the car, George."

But before George could move, a voice came from the back of the room.

"Wait!"

Everyone turned to see who had spoken.

Matt stepped forward. He felt quite embarrassed. He wasn't used to being the centre of attention. He took a deep breath and said, "He's innocent. You should let him go."

Inspector Stamp recognised the boy from earlier. He was one of the witnesses who had seen the robbery. He asked, "Where are your parents?"

"In the car park."

"Do they know you're here?"

"No, but –"

"Then you should go back to them."

"You've got to let me tell you about the thief."

"I don't *have* to do anything," said the inspector. He nodded to one of his men. "Sergeant, could you make sure this boy gets back to his parents?"

"Yes, sir." The sergeant stepped forward and put his hand on Matt's shoulder.

Shaking himself free of the sergeant's grip, Matt darted across the room and pointed at a red mark on the Duke's left hand: "What's that?"

"Are you pointing at *me*?" asked the Duke.

"I'm pointing at your left hand," said Matt. "What's that on your palm?"

"This? Oh, it's nothing."

"It's not nothing," said Matt. "It's definitely something. What is it?"

"Just a scratch. I was gardening this morning and I, um, scratched myself with a, um ... Anyway, what does it matter?"

The Duke turned to Inspector Stamp.

"What's this boy doing here? Aren't you supposed to be investigating the theft of my painting?"

"I'm sorry, my lord," said the inspector. "Sergeant!"

As the sergeant hurried forward, Matt cried out, "You've got to listen to me! Please! Or an innocent man will go to prison!"

"Come on, lad," said the sergeant, grabbing Matt with both hands.

"Let him go!" cried a voice with a strong French accent.

Everyone in the room turned to look at Véronique.

Inspector Stamp sighed. Who were all these children? And why were they disrupting his investigation? He was just about to summon another of his officers to remove this annoying girl when she said in a loud voice: "The butler has been framed!"

The inspector looked at the girl. He was struck by the determination in her voice. He knew he ought to throw her out of the room, but first he might as well hear what she had to say.

"How do you know?"

"Mathieu will explain," said Véronique.

"Oh, very well." The inspector nodded to his sergeant.

Matt stood in the centre of the room. He felt even more nervous now. He didn't even enjoy talking in front of his class at school. But he knew he couldn't back down. He held up the sticky tape so everyone could see it.

"If you analyse this piece of tape, you'll find fingerprints and DNA which will prove me right. For now, I'll just tell you how the thief did the robbery."

"This is ridiculous," said the Duke to the inspector. "Why are we listening to a little boy? May I remind you that my painting has been stolen!"

"Let's just hear what he has to say," said the inspector. He nodded to Matt. "Go on."

"If the butler were the real thief," said Matt, "he would have disguised his identity by giving himself an extra finger. But the real thief did the opposite: he disguised his identity by taping down his little finger and making it look as if he only had three fingers and a thumb on his left hand.

That was his big mistake. When he taped down his finger, a symbol was printed on the tape. The Marchmont Coat of Arms. You'll find it all over this house. You'll also find it there."

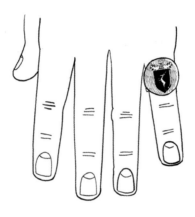

He pointed at the Duke of Marchmont's left hand. "It's printed on the signet ring that the Duke is wearing on his little finger. After the robbery, he ran into the stables, took off the mask and the gloves, and, without realising it, dropped the tape on the floor. He must have tied his finger down very tightly, because he's still got a red mark on his hand from the tape."

All eyes turned to the Duke.

For a moment, Tristram Sprockett, the nineteenth Duke of Marchmont, did not say a word. He simply stared at the small boy who was accusing him of theft.

He could have denied it, but he knew there was no point. Fingerprints and DNA would soon prove Matt right.

The Duke bowed his head. "You're quite right. I stole my own painting and framed Herbert. The Blind Horseman is insured for nine million pounds. Without that money, we're going to have to sell Marchmont Hall."

"I would have gone to prison!" cried the butler.

"Only for a few years," said the Duke with a sad smile. "My family has lived in this house for five centuries. If we don't find some money soon, we're going to lose it for ever. I couldn't let that happen."

That was when Inspector Stamp stepped in. "I'm very sorry, my lord," he said in a low voice. "I'm going to have to ask you to accompany me to the station."

The Duke submitted gracefully. He allowed himself to be led out of Marchmont Hall, down the steps and into a police car.

When the Duke had gone, the inspector and the butler turned to Matt and Véronique.

"I owe you an apology," said Inspector Stamp. "You were right and I was wrong."

"And I owe you much more," said Herbert Maples. "You've saved me from prison. How can I ever thank you?"

"Actually," said Matt, "there is one thing you could do."

An hour later, Matt, Véronique and Mr and Mrs Clarke were sitting down to the biggest cream tea that any of them had ever seen. They had cups of tea, of course, or orange juice, and cucumber sandwiches, and flapjacks, and six different kinds of cake, and, best of all, their plates were piled high with scones smothered in clotted cream and lathered with strawberry jam.

Even Véronique had to admit that she'd never tasted anything so delicious.

Matt said, "So what are you going to say to people at home who ask you about English food?"

Véronique smiled and reached for another scone. "I will say to them, 'You must try the cream tea.'"